Harcourt

Orlando Boston Dallas Chicago San Diego

Visit *The Learning Site!*
www.harcourtschool.com

This edition is published by special arrangement with Scholastic Inc.

Grateful acknowledgment is made to Scholastic Inc. for permission to reprint
The Greatest Treasure by Demi. Copyright © 1998 by Demi.
Published by Scholastic Press, a division of Scholastic Inc.

Printed in the United States of America

ISBN 0-15-314357-6

4 5 6 7 8 9 10 060 03 02

For the young
of all ages
everywhere

Long ago in China, there lived a rich man named Pang.
All day long Pang worried about his money. He counted it and sorted it.
He worried about how he should spend it
and how he could get more.

Pang had five sons.
When his sons wanted to play with him, he scowled.
"I'm much too busy!" he cried.

Then when they ran to their mother, she would say,
"Remember the great proverb, my sons.
With money you are a dragon, without it you are a worm."

Not far away lived a poor man named Li.
All day long he worked his small farm.
But whenever he had a chance,
he pulled out the flute he had made and played a merry song.

Whenever Li played his flute,
his wife and their five daughters sang and danced.
The sound of music and laughter filled the air.

Day and night, the music and laughter from Li's farm
reached Pang in his great house.
Then Pang lost count of his counting and had to begin again.
"This merriment must stop!" declared Pang.

Pang had an idea.
"If Li were rich," he thought,
"he would not have time to make so much noise."

Pang filled a large bag with money.
Then he rode in his carriage to Li's door and delivered his gift.
"I wish to share my treasure with you," said Pang to Li.
"Please take these gold coins. Use them wisely!"

Li could hardly believe his eyes.
He had never seen so many gold coins.

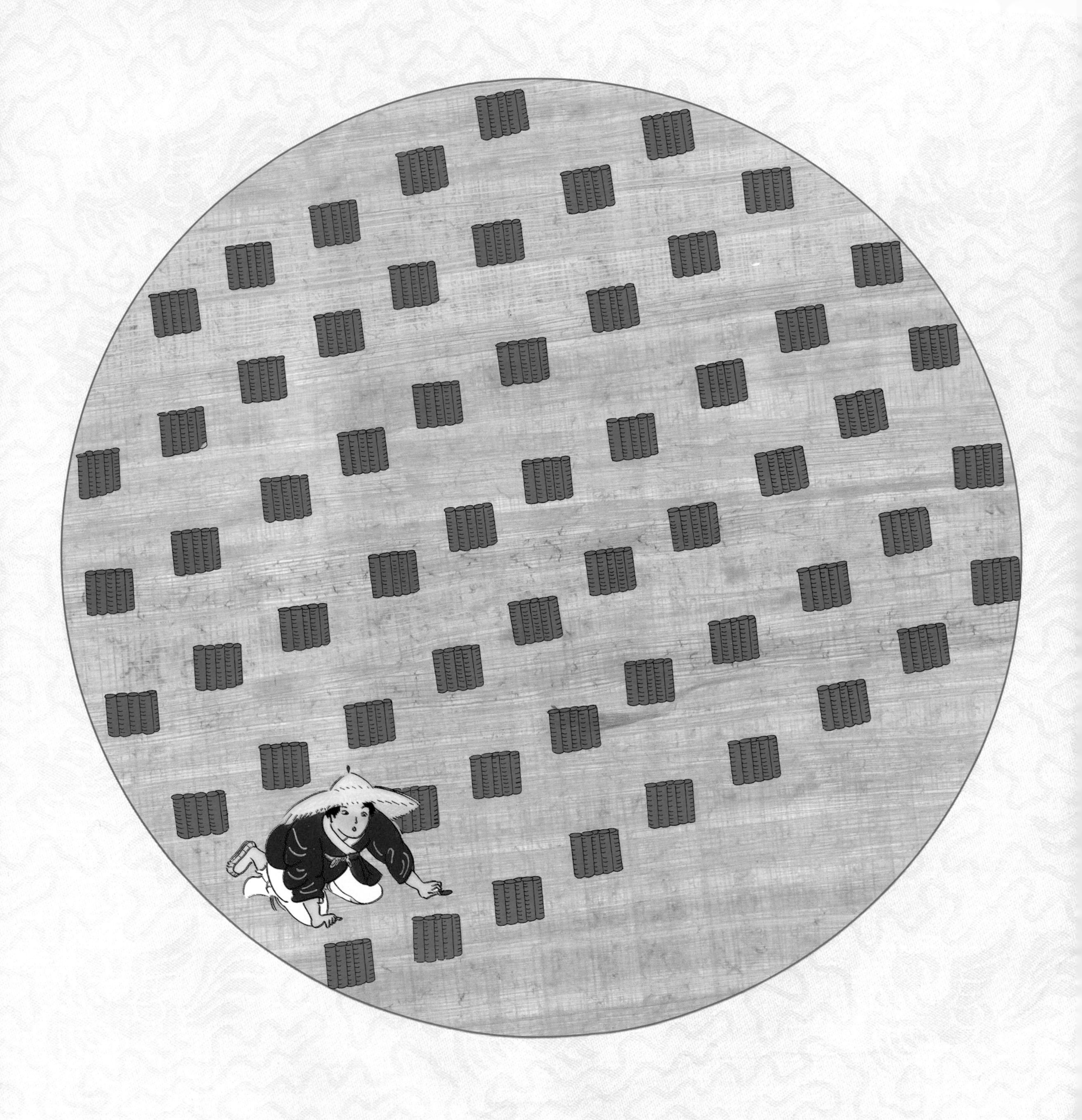

"What should I do with this money?"
wondered Li. "First I must count it."
So he set out the coins in piles on the floor,
and he counted them.

But he began to worry that he had not counted correctly.
So he counted the coins again.
Then he counted them one more time.
Before he had finished, a whole day had passed,
and he had not played his flute at all.

The next day, Li began to worry
that someone might steal the money.
"I must hide it," he said. "But where?"
First Li stuck the bag inside the stove.

Then he put it in the cellar. Then he tied it to the rafters.
Finally he dropped it into the well.
Before he had finished, another day had passed,
and Li had not played his flute at all.

The next day, Li began to worry
about how he should spend the money.
First he thought he should buy an ox.
Then he thought he should buy a plow.

Then he thought he should buy six fat hens.
Then he thought he should buy a fine robe.
Before he could think any more, another day had passed,
and Li had not played his flute at all.

The next day, Li began to worry again.
"What if I have less money than I thought?" he wondered.
So he pulled the bag up from the well and began to count the coins once more.
"Father," said the youngest girl, "won't you please play your flute,
so we can sing and dance as we used to?"

Li scowled. "I'm much too busy!" he cried.
Now he had lost count of the coins, and he had to begin again.
Then Li's wife spoke. "Remember the great proverb, my daughters.
He who has heaven in his heart is never poor."

Suddenly Li stopped counting and laughed out loud.
"Now I know what I must do with this money!" he cried.
"I must give it back!"

He kicked over the piles of coins.
Then he pulled out his flute and began to play.
Around him, his wife and daughters sang and danced,
and laughter filled the air again.

Then Li felt sorry for Pang.
He decided to present Pang with a gift,
and he worked all night till the gift was ready.

The next morning, Li and his family walked to the great house of Pang.

"I must return your gracious gift," said Li to Pang.

"This treasure almost robbed me of my happiness!"

Pang was so surprised, he couldn't say a word.

"Now please let me share my treasure with you," said Li.
And he handed Pang a package.
Inside were flutes that Li had made — one for Pang,
and one for his wife, and one for each of Pang's five sons.

Li gave flutes to his wife and five daughters, too.
Then he brought out his own flute and began to play a merry song.
Li's family cheered and began to dance and play.
Pang's wife and five sons blew into their new flutes,
and soon they too were dancing and playing merry songs.

Pang covered his ears.
"How will I keep track of my counting now?" he cried.
Then Li said, "Remember the great proverb, my friend.
Gold and silver have their price,
but peace and happiness are priceless."

Pang smiled. "You are right," he said.
Then he too began to play on the flute that Li had given him.

And now they shared . . .

the greatest treasure of all.